The BOBBSEY TWINS

Freddie and Flossie and the Train Ride

by Laura Lee Hope

illustrated by Chuck Pyle

Ready-to-Read

Aladdin

New York   London   Toronto   Sydney

Visit us at www.abdopub.com

Spotlight, a division of ABDO Publishing Company, is a school and library distributor of high quality reinforced library bound editions.

Library bound edition © 2006

Library of Congress Cataloging-in-Publication Data

Hope, Laura Lee.
Freddie and Flossie and the train ride / by Laura Lee Hope; illustrated by Chuck Pyle.—1st ed.
p. cm.—(Ready-to-Read) (Bobbsey twins)
Summary: Twins Freddie and Flossie take the train to Grandma's house with their cat Snoop.
1-4169-0269-4 (pbk.)
[1. Twins—Fiction. 2. Brothers and sisters—Fiction. 3. Cats—Fiction. 4. Railroad—Trains—Fiction.]
I. Pyle, Chuck, 1954— ill. II. Title. III. Series.
PZ7.H772Fqb 2005
[E]—dc22   2004017890
1-59961-097-3 (reinforced library bound edition)

All Spotlight books are reinforced library binding and manufactured in the United States of America

Freddie and Flossie
go to Grandma's house.

Snoop comes too.

They board the train.

They find their seats.

They give the man their tickets.

Do you want
to play, Snoop?

Oops!

Come back, Snoop!

Here, kitty kitty.

Where is Snoop?

Up there.

MEOW!

Shhh!

We are here!

Get Snoop.

Grandma!

What a nice kitten!